LUCK with POTATOES

LUCK with POTATOES

story by Helen Ketteman
illustrations by Brian Floca

ORCHARD BOOKS   NEW YORK

FOR MY MOTHER, MARY L. MOON, WHO SPENT MANY YEARS TEACHING CHILDREN TO READ
—H.K.

FOR MY SISTER ELIZABETH
—B.F.

Orchard Books, 95 Madison Avenue, New York, NY 10016

Manufactured in the United States of America. Printed by Barton Press, Inc.
Bound by Horowitz/Rae. Book design by Mina Greenstein.
The text of this book is set in 14 point Novarese Medium. The illustrations are watercolor paintings reproduced in full color.   10   9   8   7   6   5   4   3   2   1

Library of Congress Cataloging-in-Publication Data
Ketteman, Helen. Luck with potatoes / story by Helen Ketteman ; illustrations by Brian Floca.
p   cm. "A Richard Jackson book"—Half t. p.
Summary: Hardscrabble Tennessee farmer Clemmon Hardigree's hard luck changes when he plants seed potatoes in Cow Hollow before his fat mountain cows cause the pasture to collapse.
ISBN 0-531-09473-1.   ISBN 0-531-08773-5 (lib. bdg.)
[1. Potatoes—Fiction. 2. Cows—Fiction. 3. Farms—Fiction. 4. Tennessee—Fiction. 5. Tall tales.]   I. Floca, Brian, ill.
II. Title. PZ7.K494Lu 1995 [E]—dc20 94-48806

I CAN'T REMEMBER A TIME when one man in these hills came into a streak of luck like Clemmon Hardigree.

Clemmon was a hardscrabble, hard-luck farmer, barely able to scratch a living from the dirt. His farm was in the hills of Tennessee, where the hills aren't that much taller, but the hollows are a lot deeper than in most other places.

Whatever Clemmon tried, something went wrong. If a flash flood didn't wash his corn away, a rockslide buried it. Then one spring Clemmon's plow broke, and his old mule, Samantha, lay down and died of happiness. Clemmon decided to give up farming and invest his meager savings in a herd of mountain cows.

Mountain cows are bred for mountains and hills. They have holes in their ears and their back legs are longer than their front ones. Walking uphill's easy, but they can't walk back down. So when they're done grazing for the day, they tuck their back legs through the holes in their ears, form a tight ball, and roll down the mountain.

Once Clemmon got his cows, things went all right for a while. They wandered the hills until they found one really good grazing pasture. Every morning they trudged uphill to graze, and every evening they rolled back down to Clemmon's farm.

They fattened up in no time. One morning when they were grazing, the whole pasture gave way under their weight.

The cave-in was heard for miles. Clemmon and his old hound dog, Mose, went to investigate. When they arrived at what used to be the pasture, Clemmon could hardly believe his eyes. The cows were gone, and so was his pasture. In its place was one of the deepest hollows in the Tennessee hills. The locals named it Cow Hollow, and if you're ever up that way, they'll point it out to you.

Clemmon lost his entire herd of mountain cows, plus his best grazing pasture to boot. Things were looking down, but Clemmon wasn't the kind to give up.

He determined to take one more shot at farming. He spent his last few dollars on some seed potatoes, and decided to plant them up at the new hollow. It would be difficult, but the soil up there was the richest on his farm.

The next morning Clemmon took the seed potatoes, a hoe, and a length of rope, and he and Mose headed up to Cow Hollow.

Those were some steep
slopes on that hollow.
A few trees were left along the top edges,
and Clemmon tied himself and Mose to a tree
with sturdy ropes to keep from rolling down
to the bottom.

Then Clemmon set out planting.

It wasn't easy. In some places, the new hollow was so narrow he could barely squeeze through. And some places were so tight Mose had to wag his tail up and down, 'stead of sideways. Once Clemmon thought he heard a cow mooing. The hair on the back of his neck prickled. Cow Hollow must be haunted by mountain cow ghosts! Clemmon finished planting as quick as he could. He aimed to be out of there by dark.

MMMMMOOOOooo

That night it rained so hard, Clemmon couldn't hear himself snore. In the morning, he decided to check his potatoes, expecting them to be washed away. When he got there, to his surprise, the potatoes had not only held, they'd grown into ten-foot plants overnight. Looked like a regular jungle.

Those potato plants grew until they dwarfed all the trees around. Clouds got snagged in the leaves and couldn't go any farther. It created a rain forest right there in Cow Hollow.

All summer Clemmon tended his potatoes. They grew so fast they caused earthquakes. The hollow rattled and shook, bulging and growing until it plumped out into a huge, lumpy hill. The ground was stretched so tight over those potatoes, the locals figured it would blow before harvest. But Clemmon's luck held firm.

Come harvest time, the potatoes had grown so big Clemmon had to bring in a bulldozer to dig them up. The first plant he dug had potatoes so huge, each one filled the bed of his pickup. As he loaded the first one, he heard the mooing again. He leaned his ear against the potato. The mooing was coming from inside! Clemmon all but fainted. He'd grown haunted potatoes! He drove his truck to the army base twenty miles away, sold the potato for a good price, and went home. When the army cook sliced the potato, a mountain cow strolled out. Skinny as it was, it kicked its heels up and headed for Clemmon's place. Mountain cows can always find their way home.

Clemmon returned home late that night and crawled into bed. The next morning when he saw that skinny mountain cow in his front yard, he realized what had happened. He scrounged up some feed for the cow, then headed up to harvest the rest of his herd. Clemmon dug the potatoes and split them, freeing his cows.

One potato got away from him and rolled down the other side of the hollow, loosening dirt and rocks as it picked up speed. Turned out, the Army Corps of Engineers was beginning work on a dam in that very area, and the dirt and rocks piled up in one place, creating a natural dam. Saved the government a heap of money, and it sent Clemmon a fat reward check.

But that potato wasn't done. It rolled on through a mountain, creating a nice-sized tunnel. Clemmon thought he was in trouble for that, but his luck had changed, all right. He soon learned the state was going to build a road out that way, and, as luck would have it, they planned to tunnel through that very mountain. Clemmon collected another reward for saving the state all that work and expense.

The Tennessee Rag

Potato Performs Public Works Projects

Farmer Honored, Unions Protest

The Potato

Spud Stud

And that potato still wasn't done. It rolled to the bottom of Morgan's Gap and up to the top of Eagle Mountain on the other side of the gap, mowing down trees in its path. It reached the top, then rolled back down again. That potato rolled up and down Morgan's Gap for days. By the time it stopped, there wasn't a tree left standing.

The timber in Morgan's Gap was owned by Angus Mayfield, known throughout the hills as the stingiest man around. Angus's reputation being what it was, Clemmon thought he'd have to pay Angus all his reward money and then some to cover the loss of the trees.

Clemmon's luck was still holding, though. Angus had just signed a contract to sell the trees in Morgan's Gap to a timber company. He was so tickled he didn't have to hire loggers to cut them down, he gave Clemmon a crisp five-dollar bill.

When the potato finally came to rest, it filled in a swamp Angus had been wanting to fill for some time. He allowed Clemmon to go in and drill for his cow, which he found and took home, but the potato stayed put. It wasn't too long before that potato started petrifying, and old Angus plans to mine gravel there in a few more years.

By the time Clemmon finished saving all his cows, he had a
mountain range of potato chunks. He sawed them into planks and sold
them to a lumber company.

It's been a lot of years since then, and Clemmon still has his herd of mountain cows. They found another, sturdier pasture to graze in, and haven't had any trouble since.

Clemmon still plants potatoes up in Cow Hollow, too. 'Course, over the years, the soil has become a little less fertile. His last crop of potatoes was down in size to where he could fit three at a time into the bed of his pickup. Still and all, that Clemmon Hardigree has had a dang good streak of luck with potatoes.

He surely has.